IR

D0629618

HELLO, I'M THEA!

I'm *Geronimo Stilton*'s sister. As I'm sure you know from my brother's bestselling novels, I'm a special correspondent for *The Rodent's Gazette,* Mouse Island's most famouse newspaper. Unlike my 'fraidy mouse brother, I absolutely adore traveling, having adventures, and meeting rodents from all around the world!

The adventure I want to tell you about begins at Mouseford Academy, the school I went to when I was a young mouseling. I had such a great experience there as a student that I came back to teach a journalism class.

When I returned as a grown mouse, I met five really special students: Colette, Nicky, Pamela, Paulina, and Violet. You could hardly imagine five more different mouselings, but they became great friends right away. And they liked me so much that they decided to name their group after me: the Thea Sisters! I was so touched by that, I decided to write about their adventures. So turn the page to read a fabumouse adventure about the

THEA SISTERS!

Colette

She has a passion for clothing and style, especially anything pink. When she grows up, she wants to be a fashion editor.

Paulina

Cheerful and kind, she loves traveling and meeting rodents from all over the world. She has a magic touch when it comes to technology.

Violet

She's the bookworm of the group, and she loves learning. She enjoys classical music and dreams of becoming a famouse violinist.

THE THEA SISTERS

Nicky

She comes from Australia and is very enthusiastic about sports and nature. She loves being outside and is always ready to get up and go!

Pamela

She is a great mechanic: Give her a screwdriver and she'll fix anything! She loves pizza, which she eats every day, and she loves to cook.

Do you want to help the Thea Sisters in this new adventure? It's not hard — just follow the clues!

When you see this magnifying glass, pay attention: It means there's an important clue on the page. Each time one appears, we'll review the clues so we don't miss anything.

ARE YOU READY?
A NEW MYSTERY AWAITS!

Geronimo Stilton

Thea Stilton
AND THE FROZEN FIASCO

Scholastic Inc.

Published by Scholastic Inc., *Publishers since 1920*, 557 Broadway, New York, NY 10012. SCHOLASTIC and associated logos are trademarks and/or registered trademarks of Scholastic Inc.

ISBN 978-1-338-08786-4

Text by Thea Stilton
Original title *Inseguimento tra i ghiacci*
Cover by Caterina Giorgetti (design) and Flavio Ferron (color)
Illustrations by Barbara Pellizzari and Chiara Balleello (design), Valeria Cairoli (color base), and Valentina Grassini (color)
Graphics by Elena Dal Maso

Special thanks to Beth Dunfey
Translated by Emily Clement
Interior design by Becky James

10 9 8 7 6 5 4 3 2 1 17 18 19 20 21

Printed in the U.S.A. 40
First printing 2017

DISAPPEARING STUDENTS

At Mouseford Academy, the spring semester was winding down. It was time for Headmaster Octavius de Mousus to deliver his **traditional** end-of-term speech. He straightened his **BOW TIE** and strode into the **GREAT HALL**, but it was **deserted**!

The headmaster stared at the empty seats in dismay. Where were all the students?

Just then, the school handymouse, Boomer Whale, scurried in with a **huge** mop.

"Headmaster! What in the name of **string cheese** are you doing in here?" he asked.

"I was supposed to squeak to the students," the headmaster said. "Where are they?"

Boomer smiled. "Oh, you haven't heard?

The Volcano Chase hits stores today! After *Mystery on Ice*, the students just can't wait for the next installment."

"**Volcano? ICE?** What are you talking about?" the headmaster asked.

"You know, the latest masterpiece from Vígmar Ratsson, the great **mystery** writer," Boomer explained. "Haven't you heard of him? His books are total page-turners! I was

up all NIGHT reading the last one."

"Um . . . I . . . actually, I don't know who he is. And I don't understand what that has to do with my STUDENTS disappearing," the headmaster said grumpily.

Boomer chuckled. "Headmaster, do I really need to spell it out for you? They all scampered off to the bookstore to get their copies!"

Curious, the headmaster headed for the school bookstore. A crowd of students had gathered outside, including the THEA SISTERS — best friends Colette, Nicky, Pam, Paulina, and Violet.

"Headmaster, I didn't know you were a fan of Vígmar Ratsson," exclaimed Violet. "Have you come to get a copy of The Volcano Chase?"

"To be honest, I just heard about the book

about five minutes ago. But it must be pretty compelling reading to make everyone forget our assembly in the Great Hall," the headmaster replied sternly.

Violet gasped and turned redder than a cheese rind. "Oh, the end-of-term speech!"

"OH NO! We forgot!" Pamela said.

"We're very sorry . . ." Colette added.

"It's just that the book is HOT off the presses, and we couldn't wait to get our paws on it," Paulina chimed in.

The headmaster smiled. "Oh, it's all right. What kind of headmaster would I be if I complained about my students reading? But perhaps this means . . ."

The mouselets exchanged a worried LOOK: Was the headmaster thinking up a punishment for them?

". . . that I should pick up a few BOOKS

Vigmar Ratsson
THE VOLCANO CHASE
THE NEW BOOK FROM ICELAND'S BESTSELLING AUTHOR!
Uh-oh, we completely forgot!

by this author myself," the headmaster concluded.

The Thea Sisters burst out laughing.

"**You'll go gaga for his stuff, you'll see!**" Pam said. "Ratsson's mysteries will make your heart race. And you'll love the setting — it takes place in the author's homeland, **Iceland**!"

Violet nodded. "That's right. We've learned so much about Iceland's **amazing** volcanoes and geysers and glaciers."

"Start with the first book, *The Case of the Silver Waterfall*," Colette suggested. "That's the one where Inspector Ólafur investigates a **mysterious** art thief who has a secret hideaway under —"

"Stop, stop!" the headmaster interrupted her. "Don't spoil it! I want to **solve** the mystery myself . . . Otherwise, where's the fun?"

MYSTERY WEDNESDAYS

When the Thea Sisters first started reading Ratsson's **novels**, they came up with an idea for a book club called "Mystery Wednesdays." Every **Wednesday evening**, the mouselets gathered in Pam and Colette's room to discuss the chapters they'd read, try to **GUESS** who the culprit was, and share their favorite passages.

That night, the **mouselets** were seated on the floor with their books in their paws.

"When **Inspector** Ólafur climbed the volcano and hid inside that crevice, I was so nervous I almost **JUMPED** out of my fur," Paulina cried.

"Me, too!" Colette agreed, nodding

vigorously. "Someone drew him into a trap with a **text message**, but who?"

"It's clear the inspector is involved in a case that's way **BIGGER** than he realized . . ." Violet commented. Her tone suggested she knew more than she was saying.

"Vi, don't tell me you've read **AHEAD**! We agreed we'd stop after the third chapter."

Colette groaned, frowning.

Violet turned bright pink. "**BUSTED!** Sorry, mouselets, I just couldn't wait."

Colette laughed. "Okay, okay, but no spoilers, all right?"

"Volcanoes, frozen waterfalls, fjords," Nicky said dreamily. "Iceland must be a MAGICAL place to visit." Nicky loved exploring and the outdoors.

Paulina agreed. "Do you remember Roska and Arna, the sisters from **Iceland** we met last summer? You know, when Mouseford hosted that summit for students around the world? Arna showed us pictures of places that sounded like the ones described in the Inspector Ólafur books."

"Maybe they read Ratsson's **mysteries**, too," Colette said.

"We could ask them," Paulina suggested,

reaching for her laptop. "Let's send them an email!"

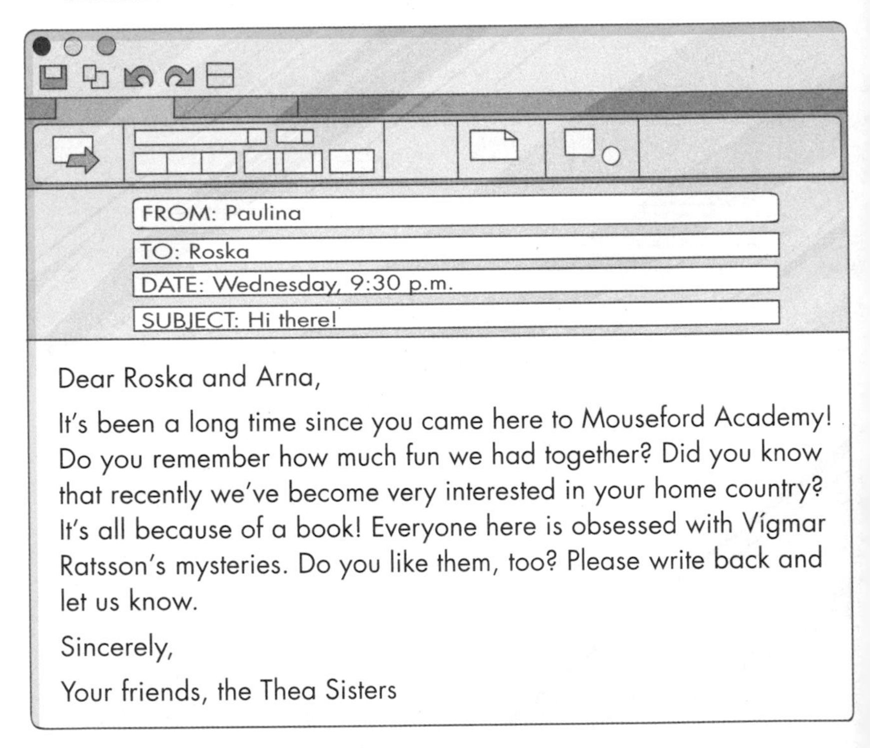
FROM: Paulina

TO: Roska

DATE: Wednesday, 9:30 p.m.

SUBJECT: Hi there!

Dear Roska and Arna,

It's been a long time since you came here to Mouseford Academy! Do you remember how much fun we had together? Did you know that recently we've become very interested in your home country? It's all because of a book! Everyone here is obsessed with Vígmar Ratsson's mysteries. Do you like them, too? Please write back and let us know.

Sincerely,

Your friends, the Thea Sisters

Violet **yawned**. "Is anyone else sleepy?"

"Yep, I'm wiped," Paulina replied, scrambling to her paws. "Let's turn in. Maybe we'll have an answer by morning."

The next morning when Paulina turned on her computer to check her email, she let out a cheer.

"What's going on, Paulina?" asked Violet.

"Look!" her friend cried, pointing to the screen. "Roska and Arna already replied!"

FROM: Roska

TO: Paulina

DATE: Thursday, 8:00 a.m.

SUBJECT: RE: Hi there!

Dear Thea Sisters,

It was so nice to receive your message! And what a surprise to hear about your favorite books!!! We know Inspector Ólafur, and we also know his author. You see, Vígmar Ratsson is our uncle!

When your semester is over, would you like to spend your break here in Iceland? Our uncle is going on tour to all the bookstores in the capital, Reykjavík. You could come meet him in the fur!

Write back soon,

R&A

The **MOUSELETS** couldn't believe it. Were they really going to get to meet their *favorite* author?

"Sisters, what do you think?" Pam asked.

The Thea Sisters looked at one another. Each mouselet was **nodding** in agreement.

Colette answered for all of them. "Okay, then get out your heaviest sweaters, hats, and wool gloves.

ICELAND

Iceland is an island nation in Europe. Surrounded by the **Atlantic Ocean**, it is largely covered in **glacier ice** and **cooled lava**. The landscape is dotted with glaciers, volcanoes, and lava fields that have formed over many centuries.

The first people to reach Iceland were **Irish monks** looking for a place to pray without interruption. They formed the first settlements in the eighth century CE. The first **Viking settlers** arrived around 874 CE. The Vikings founded the first villages (including the capital, **Reykjavík**) and began to develop Icelandic sagas — tales that told the history of the land.

A WARM WELCOME!

A week later, when the Thea Sisters **landed** in Reykjavík, Roska and Arna hurried to hug their friends. The two sisters from Iceland were **happier** than mice in a cupboard filled with cheese. They immediately began peppering the mouselets with questions.

"Did you have a good trip?"

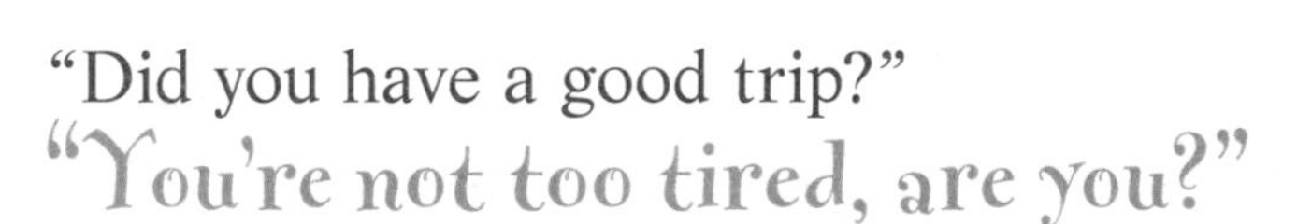

"You're not too tired, are you?"

"Because we were thinking we'd take you out for a treat . . ."

". . . and then a quick **scamper** around the city . . ."

". . . before bringing you to the bookstore to **meet our uncle**!"

The Thea Sisters looked at one another in a daze. They were exhausted from their flight, but how could they say no when their friends were so **excited** to see them?

After stopping by Arna and Roska's house to drop off their luggage and snack on some **kleinur** (tasty Icelandic doughnuts), all seven mouselets piled into a car and headed into **town**.

Arna drove them along the **STREETS** of Reykjavík. The Thea Sisters gazed out the windows and admired the countryside, which was dominated by a **snowy** mountain.

"That's Mount Esja," Roska explained. "It's not very tall, but isn't it majestic?"

"Here we are!" Arna said. "The **city** was built on Faxa Bay. We call it Faxaflói. We can walk along the coastline, and you can tell us all the **news** from Mouseford."

As they scurried along, Violet noticed a building made of GLASS. "Why, that's the Harpa!" she exclaimed. "It's the city's CONCERT HALL."

Soon the mouselets had reached the shores of a small lake. "This is Tjörnin," Arna explained.

And here's Tjörnin!

"Seriously? This is where **INSPECTOR ÓLAFUR** goes to think about his cases," Paulina cried. "I can see why! This place is fabumouse."

Roska smiled. "Yep, this is it. Now let's go. The bookstore that's throwing a party for our **UNCLE** is just over there."

The mouselets scurried over to a large shop with neat piles of Vígmar Ratsson's latest **BOOK** stacked in the window.

"This is so exciting!" Colette cried. "I can't wait to get his **autograph**."

"We'll go out to **eat** together after the event," Arna said. "So you can ask him all your questions."

"**YES!** Uncle Vígmar will be very happy to squeak with you," Roska agreed. "Come on, we'd better go in. The reading is about to begin!"

A LONG WAIT

Paulina was so eager to meet her favorite writer that she scampered ahead of her friends. But before she could go into the store, a ratlet in a **DARK** uniform blocked her path.

"**Let them through**," the ratlet commanded, signaling for a gentlemouse and an elegant rodent to go in ahead of the mouselets.

"What's up with that?" Paulina murmured. She was surprised by the ratlet's pushy behavior.

Roska joined her. "They're Gustav and Irma, the owners of Lundi Publishing, our uncle's publisher," she explained in a low squeak.

"Rumor has it they're both very difficult rodents, but they really know how to make a book **successful**," Arna explained.

It was getting **CROWDED**. Colette found herself next to a mouselet clutching a purple PORTFOLIO. She was staring at the stage anxiously.

"It's so exciting to see such a famouse writer in the fur, right?" Colette asked her neighbor.

The mouselet shrugged. "I squeak with him all the time. I'm his **editor**," she replied. She made her way through the crowd and stood next to the two publishers in front of the stage.

"Mouselets, what exactly does a book editor do?" Colette asked as she sat down with her friends in the second row.

"Doesn't it sound like a fun job?" Roska said. "The editor is the rodent who chooses which BOOKS to publish and helps writers make their stories better. Tomorrow, our uncle has to send his editor, Bryndís, the manuscript for his next novel, *Black Tide.* It's a new story about INSPECTOR ÓLAFUR."

Paulina lit up. "Do you know what it's about? I'm so curious!"

Her friend shook her snout. "No. Uncle Vígmar **always** keeps what he's writing about a secret. He enjoys the suspense."

"All we know is that he's done a lot of research," Arna added. "He just returned from his latest trip, which was **key** to the final chapters of his new book."

Just then, a ratlet scurried over. He practically **tripped** over his tail before

collapsing into an empty chair next to the two sisters.

"Stefán! Scampering in at the last minute as usual," Roska scolded him.

"I had to go back home because I forgot this," Stefán explained, pulling out his copy of *The Volcano Chase*. "At least I didn't miss anything. I was afraid I was going to be SUPER late!"

"No, you're just super distracted!" Arna said jokingly. "Can't you see we have company?"

Oof! That was a close one!

The ratlet's EYES turned to the Thea Sisters. "Of course! You must be the mice from Mouseford. I'm Stefán. I go to

school with these two sweet sisters," he said, shaking paws with Colette, Nicky, Pam, Paulina, and **Violet**.

Roska rolled her eyes. "Stefán is more charming than a chinchilla! He loves teasing us." She gave Stefán a playful SHOVE.

"Pleasure to meet you, Stefán," Paulina replied. "Are you a fan of Vígmar Ratsson, too?"

Stefán nodded. "Yes, I've read all his books. I can't wait to meet him."

Arna looked around thoughtfully. "It's weird that Uncle isn't here yet . . . It's not like him to be late."

"Let's hope he hurries. Everyone's getting restless," said Roska.

It was true. Many rodents in the audience were murmuring, and a few were looking around for the famouse author.

Colette heard Gustav whisper to Irma, "Where could Ratsson be?"

"These authors are such a pain in the tail. They're completely unreliable!" Irma replied.

Another half hour passed, and finally the BOOKSTORE CLERK went up to the microphone. "Thank you all for coming tonight," she began, "but I'm afraid that we have to cancel the event. Vígmar Ratsson hasn't arrived, and no one has been able to contact him."

A chorus of surprised and disappointed squeaks rose up in the room.

The Thea Sisters exchanged a worried look: What could have happened to their friends' uncle?

A MYSTERIOUS DISAPPEARANCE

Roska dialed her uncle's cell phone, but then she shook her snout. "His phone is turned off."

"You don't think something happened to him, do you?" Arna said.

"He probably just got **STUCK** in traffic or something," said Paulina.

"Paulina's right," Violet said. "Maybe his cell phone is dead."

"If only I had a piece of cheese for every time that happened to me," Colette said, nodding. "I'm sure he'll call back soon."

But Arna shook her snout. "You don't know Uncle Vígmar. He's the most PRECISE rodent in all of Reykjavík. He'd NEVER get

stuck in traffic before a reading or let his cell battery run down."

"It's true," Roska confirmed. "He never misses an event without letting someone know."

Just then, a rodent who'd been WATCHING them approached the mouselets and their friends.

"I couldn't help overhearing you call Vígmar Ratsson 'uncle,'" the rodent remarked. "Do I have the HONOR of squeaking with relatives of the most famouse writer in Iceland?"

Roska and Arna exchanged glances. "Yes, we are his nieces. And you are . . . ?"

"Do you mean to squeak you don't recognize Orri, the most infamouse journalist in Reykjavík?" said Bryndís, joining the group.

THE VOLCANO CHASE
THE NEW BOOK
Where could Uncle Vígmar be?

“**Thank you** for your kind words,” the rodent replied, bowing his snout.

“Oh, don’t mention it. I always recognize journalists who have reputations . . . even if the reputation is only for gossip!” Bryndís replied acidly.

Orri was squeakless for a moment. By the time he could think of a reply, Ratsson’s editor had **scampered off**.

The journalist turned his attention back to Roska and Arna. “Where were we? Oh, yes, you were telling me about your uncle’s next triumph.”

“I — we weren’t telling you anything. We don’t know anything about it!” Roska replied.

“But I can’t believe that your uncle would keep secrets from such **DELIGHTFUL** nieces,” Orri said coaxingly.

The mouselets **shook** their snouts.

"At least tell me what Ólafur's next case will be," Orri went on. "How about the beginning of the first chapter . . . or maybe the last line?"

"But . . . what . . . we can't . . ." stammered Arna, confused.

"We're not giving you an **interview**!" Roska snapped.

Stefán put his paw around his friends' shoulders. "Scamper off and find a **SCOOP** somewhere else!" he told Orri.

The *journalist* tried to interject, but the Thea Sisters blocked his path. So

Orri gave up and headed toward the bookseller.

Outside the bookstore, the friends huddled together to come up with a PLAN.

Roska was checking her cell phone again. "I just texted my parents and cousins, and they don't know anything, either. **No one** has heard from him in the last few days. That's pretty normal when he's finishing up a new novel. But forgetting about a reading . . . that's not normal. Not normal at all."

Paulina squeezed her friend's paw.

A BITTER SURPRISE

Arna buried her snout in her paws. When she looked up again, her eyes were shining with tears. "Poor Uncle. Where could he be?"

"There's no reason to lose hope." Colette reassured her, putting a paw on her shoulder.

"Colette is right," Stefán agreed. "First, let's go by his house and see if he's there or if he's left any CLUES."

"I'm sure we can find him if we work together," Violet said. "We Thea Sisters are here to help."

"Well said, Sis!" Pam CRIED.

Arna wiped her eyes with the back of her paw. "Okay, let's go," she said, smiling at her friends gratefully.

They all piled back into the car. Roska took a street that led AWAY from the center of Reykjavík.

"Where does your uncle live?" asked Paulina.

"Just outside the CITY, in a house in the hills," Arna replied.

"He says he needs silence and tranquility to concentrate on his writing," Roska explained.

After a few minutes, the car left the last of the big city buildings behind. They stopped in front of a small WOODEN house. Its roof was covered in a layer of thick green grass.

"CRUSTY CHEESE CHUNKS!" cried Pam.

We're here!

"Um, why is there a hill on top of your uncle's house?!"

Arna smiled. "Our uncle renovated this old farmhouse. Isn't it cool? The GRASS on the roof insulates the house and keeps in the HEAT."

"Wow!" said Nicky, joining them. "That's a great idea. It's so eco-friendly!"

Colette was heading for the door when she was stopped by a sudden thought. "But . . . if your uncle isn't **home**, how will we get in?"

Roska winked. "No problem. We know where he keeps the **KEY**. Come on!"

She led the group to a large **BOULDER** along the house's front path.

"Don't tell me it's under that," said Colette in **SURPRISE**. "That boulder is enormouse; it'd take a real musclemouse to lift it!"

"Oh, no worries. We don't need to LIFT it,"

Arna reassured her. "Since you're such big fans of Uncle's books, you won't be surprised to hear he loves puzzles and riddles. There's a **SECRET** to the key's hiding place. You just need to recognize the key."

"The **KEY** to the house? Or the **KEY** to the hiding place?" Pam asked, confused. "I don't get it at all!"

Roska gave her a **crafty** look. "That's just because you're not used to Uncle Vígmar! Did you notice these?" She pointed to the bottom of the rock.

Pam looked down. There were three **MUSHROOMS** growing at the boulder's base.

"This is the

third house you pass outside the **CITY**. Therefore, to find the key, you just have to do *this*," Roska explained. She **stretched** her paw toward the third mushroom, pressed it down into the ground, and suddenly . . .

CLICK!

A mechanism clicked, and a tiny window in the boulder popped open.

"**Holey cheese**, it's the key!" cried Pam.

"So clever," Violet said, patting the stone. "It's the **perfect puzzle**."

"And the perfect spot for the key to a mystery writer's house," Colette said.

With the key in paw, the mouselets scurried up to the front door. There they found an unfortunate surprise.

"Uh-oh, mouselets . . ." Paulina groaned. "It looks like we won't need the key after all . . ."

THE DOOR WAS HALF-OPEN!

"Someone picked the lock!" Stefán cried.

"Let's be careful," Roska said. "I have a bad feeling about this . . ."

The inside of the house was **DARK**. The young mice peered in for a moment, and then Arna flipped the light switch.

The house had been completely **RANSACKED**. Every drawer and cabinet in the living room had been flung open.

Papers, **BROKEN** boxes, books, and objects of every kind were strewn across the floor.

The other rooms in the house were in the same state. Ratsson's bed was unmade, and even the kitchen was a mess!

Arna stifled a sob. "**WHO COULD HAVE DONE THIS?**"

"Someone looking for the manuscript for Vígmar Ratsson's next book," Roska replied grimly.

What happened here?
Who could have done this?

CAREFUL CLUES!

The mouselets and Stefán gazed at Roska with alarm.

"Why do you say that?" asked Colette.

Roska shrugged. "Our uncle doesn't have a lot of valuables. But the manuscript for *Black Tide* is worth a lot! He always keeps his work safe."

"Maybe someone wanted to publish the book early, or steal it and blackmail our uncle," Arna suggested, her voice shaking.

Stefán sighed. "You're probably right . . ." He picked a book up off the floor and placed it on a bookstand. "But that doesn't explain where your uncle is."

"That's true," Roska replied. "We don't even know where he was last SEEN . . ."

"Don't get down in the snout, okay?" Paulina said. "Let's LOOK around. Maybe we'll find some clues."

"Good idea," Colette agreed.

The mouselets and Stefán split up. But half an hour later, no one had found anything.

Violet paced, thinking. "The title of his new manuscript is *Black Tide*, right?"

"Yes, the title is the ONLY thing we know," said Arna.

Violet picked up the book that Stefán had placed on the bookstand. "What's this?" she asked.

"Oh, that's just a book about the geography of Iceland. Uncle Vígmar often consults it while he writes," Roska replied.

Violet had an idea. "You said that your **UNCLE** loved mysteries, so what if we try to find the word tide in this book? It might lead to something!"

Arna flipped through the **HUGE** book. When she'd reached the page about tides, she cried, "There's a **note**! And there are some numbers written here . . ."

"But what do these **NUMBERS** have to do with his manuscript?" Roska wondered.

"And do you have any idea what this **note** means? About the elf?" Violet asked.

"It sounds like part of a **FAIRY TALE** Uncle used to tell us," Arna replied.

It's just an ordinary reference book . . .

The elf balled his hands into fists and blew on them gently. When he opened his hands again, a piece of gold had appeared . . .

9 – 8
53 – 14
78 – 6

"Is there a book of **FAIRY TALES** here anywhere? This might be a **CLUE** your uncle left just for you!" Violet explained.

Arna glanced over the shelves and then pawed her friend a battered old volume.

"**LOOK!**" said Violet, opening the book to page nine, which matched the first **NUMBER** on the note. She pointed to the eighth word on the page. "*Inside . . .*"

NICKY GOT IT IMMEDIATELY. "Of course!

Hmmm...

I think it's a clue!

The first numbers indicate the pages, and the second tells the words."

Violet nodded. "If we put them **together**, they'll form a message."

A moment later, the mouselets had decoded the message: "*Inside the refrigerator.*"

The **friends** scampered into the kitchen, and Pam stuck her snout into the fridge. After she'd pushed aside a few cartons of *skyr,* a traditional **Icelandic** yogurt, she emerged with a wooden box.

"Moldy mozzarella!" she cried. "Your uncle sure knows a thing about clues . . . and awesome hiding places!"

A SECRET ALMOST REVEALED

Pam tried to open the BOX, but no matter how hard she tried, she couldn't. It was stuck.

"Look, there's a **COMBINATION LOCK**!" cried Paulina, pointing to the lid, which had a metal cylinder with numbers engraved on it.

"It's like the LOCK to my suitcase," Colette said. "It opens with a sequence of numbers that I chose myself . . ."

"But there are **FIVE DIGITS**. How will we guess the right ones? There are infinite

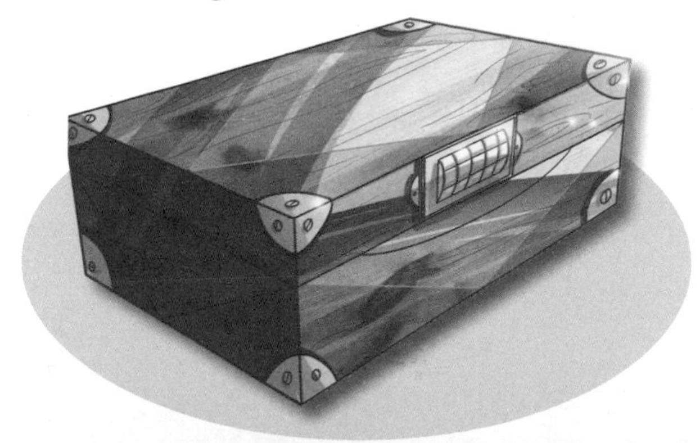

combinations!" Arna said despairingly.

Violet leaned over the box to examine it. "That's strange. Some of the digits are lined up perfectly, and one seems to be half-turned."

Stefán took a close look at the lock. "Maybe we don't need to figure out the combination . . . Maybe your uncle already SET UP the combination and just left one digit —"

"For us to figure out!" Roska said. "That sounds like Uncle Vígmar."

Paulina sat down on a pillow. "Then let's see . . . EIGHT . . . SIX . . . FOUR . . . TWO . . ." she began muttering.

"Figured something out?" Pam asked, curious.

"The missing number is ZERO," Paulina cried triumphantly.

Everyone was struck squeakless. "How do you know that?"

"Easy! It's a simple mathematic **pattern**. Think about it: The numbers all go down by two. Eight, six, four, two . . . The next number in the sequence has to be zero!" Paulina replied.

"GREASY CAT GUTS, you're a genius!" said Pam as Paulina spun the number. The lock opened with a **CLICK**.

Paulina raised her snout and looked at her friends. "Are you ready?"

They all nodded. In a moment, they would **uncover** the manuscript that half the world was waiting for!

Paulina carefully raised the lid and pulled out the box's contents.

"A NOTEBOOK?" Colette said, confused.

"Maybe the *manuscript* is inside?" Pam asked.

"That's not just any notebook — it's our

UNCLE'S journal," Arna said, taking out the little leather notebook. It was TIED shut with a leather band.

"He writes down phrases and ideas to use in his writing," Arna explained. "His research, works of art that inspire him, stuff like that . . ."

"Did you say *research*?" Paulina said. "Maybe this book contains CLUES that will help us retrace your uncle's pawsteps!"

ANOTHER ENIGMA!

Everyone leaned over to examine the little notebook.

"But . . . the pages are all BLANK," Roska squeaked.

"Not all of them. There are some words in the back," Nicky observed, opening the journal to the only page with writing. "Is this in your language?"

Stefán shook his snout. "No. It's not Icelandic."

"It looks like gibberish," Arna said.

"This is classic Uncle Vígmar. He's always adored word games," Roska put in.

The friends examined the message.

Stefán scratched his snout. "Wow, your uncle is a real riddler!"

HP XIFSF
UIF TFBHVMM TUBZT ESZ
CFOFBUI B CMBOLFU
UIBU BMXBZT GMPXT.

Arna sighed. "He's made this puzzle harder than a block of aged cheddar!"

"It's okay. I'm sure we'll be able to decipher the message," Violet said.

"How?" Roska asked.

"With teamwork!" Colette said, smiling. "After all, 'TEAMWORK makes the dream work!'"

"Maybe it's a foreign language," Pam said. "Paulina, can you check your tablet?"

"I'll look in the universal dictionary . . ." Paulina began. "Never mind, the words don't belong to a single known language."

"Maybe it's an anagram,"* said Arna.

The friends **TRIED** to create new words by rearranging the letters, but it was hopeless.

"Perhaps it's a **code**," Paulina said. "The letters could be chosen according to a system, like in the sequence we used to unlock the box."

* An anagram is a word or phrase in which the letters are rearranged to create a new word or phrase.

"There aren't any NUMBERS to add or subtract . . ." Roska protested.

"But we can make substitutions," Stefán said. "Let's try to exchange each letter with the one after it in the alphabet."

But the message still made no sense.

"What if it's the letter before instead of after?" Colette asked. She began writing:

GO WHERE
THE SEAGULL STAYS DRY
BENEATH A BLANKET
THAT ALWAYS FLOWS.

"Hooray! You did it, Coco!" Pam cheered, hugging her friend.

Stefán was confused. "But I don't get it . . . What does it mean?"

"I haven't got a clue," said Roska.

AS VOLATILE AS A VOLCANO

"Wait, I have an idea!" Paulina exclaimed. She **knocked** a few times on the bottom of the box. "I knew it! It has a **false** bottom!"

Her friends' snouts were hanging open like a pack of hungry cats at feeding time. They couldn't **BELIEVE** Paulina had figured that out.

"How did you know?" Colette asked.

"From Ratsson's novels, of course! Remember the final chapter of *Shivers in the Sunshine*, when the **INSPECTOR** found the lost will in the false bottom of Mrs. Lyrrel's dresser?"

"You're brainier than a lab rat, Paulina!" cried Pam.

"Thanks, Sis," Paulina said. She **removed** the box's bottom and pulled out a notebook page. It held a message scrawled in pen.

"It's Uncle's writing!" Arna cried. She read aloud:

I've found something truly serious. Sometimes my fiction comes too close to reality. I could be in danger, but I cannot give up my story. So I must leave to investigate and uncover the truth.

If you are the one to find this, I ask you: Solve the puzzles, reach the first landmark, and follow the clues. You'll find the story. I trust my readers' instincts to put the clues together and make good use of them.

"Landmarks . . . CLUES . . . story . . . What's he talking about?" Stefán asked Roska and Arna.

The two sisters were too shaken to reply at once. Roska began PACING around the room. "What do we do?" she murmured.

The THEA SISTERS shared a look. They knew what they had to do — help their friends. And the best way to do that was to stay calm and come up with a PLAN.

"UNCLE is in danger!" Arna sobbed.

Colette placed a paw on her shoulder. "First of all, we're not certain that he's in DANGER, and worrying won't help us or him."

"Coco's right!" Violet agreed. "Instead, we need to come up with a plan."

Paulina pulled up a map of Iceland on her tablet. "Ratsson talked about landmarks to follow . . ."

"Uncle does a lot of research while writing his books. He took many trips this time, and he probably wrote a piece of the manuscript at each stop," she explained.

"Then we must find the clues, solve them, and follow his route," Violet concluded.

"Yes. But meanwhile, who knows what kind of DANGER Uncle's gotten himself into," Arna said. "He can be as volatile as a volcano when he's got something on his mind . . ."

"Keep calm and scurry on," said Pam, smiling at Roska.

"Let's start by deciphering the first clue: the message about the seagull," Nicky

suggested. "Does that mean anything to you?"

Roska and Arna shook their snouts.

"How can a blanket flow?" asked Colette. "I'm totally lost here, mouselings! I can't see the cheese for the holes."

Paulina laughed. "Actually, Coco, you might be onto something with that cheese metaphor! I think Ratsson was using a metaphor, too — an image that represents something else. He's probably referring to something that FLOWS, but not a real blanket . . ."

"A WATERFALL! It's like a blanket, and it flows!" cried Violet.

"And it's dry behind waterfalls," Pam put in. "But what does a waterfall have to do with a **seagull**?"

"GULLFOSS!" shouted Stefán. "At

Gullfoss, there's a waterfall with a ROCK behind it — and it's shaped like a seagull!"

"Then that's where we'll go," Colette declared. She glanced at her watch. "It's already getting dark. Let's get a good night's rest, and we'll start our **INVESTIGATION** first thing tomorrow."

I can hardly keep my eyes open!

"Right on, Sis!" Pam said, yawning. "I'm so tired, I can hardly keep my eyes open."

OFF ON AN ADVENTURE!

The next day, Colette, Nicky, Pam, Paulina, Violet, Roska, and Arna woke up early and started packing their bags. Stefán was on his way to pick them up in his enormouse SUV, as they'd agreed the night before.

Violet and Pam helped Arna get the supplies ready, while Roska gave Paulina, Colette, and Nicky a paw choosing warm, comfortable clothes for the journey ahead of them.

"Sweaters, pants, warm socks . . ." Colette listed as they filled their backpacks.

"Not exactly a wardrobe off the **runway**, eh, Colette?" Nicky joked.

"The most important thing is that the clothes suit the situation," Colette replied. She was famouse for her **passion for fashion**. "Of course, if I had known that we were headed out into the wilderness, I would have packed some **cuter** sweaters . . ." she admitted in a low squeak as she placed one of Roska's **BULKY** pullovers in her backpack.

"Take these, too," Roska said, pawing her friends a bunch of scuffed-up boots. "They're a little old, but they'll be just right for **hiking**."

Nicky grinned. "Great! I've dreamed of hiking through **Iceland** since I was just a little mouseling."

"Remember that we're here to solve a

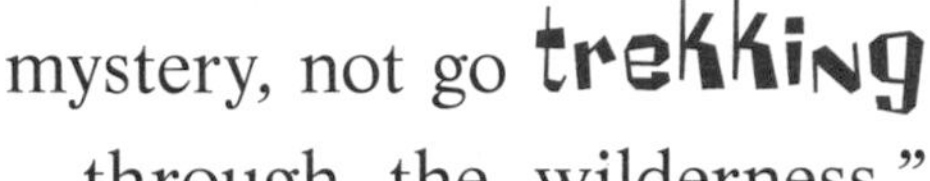

mystery, not go **trekking** through the wilderness," Colette muttered. There were a lot more **SIGHTS** she'd hoped to see in Reykjavík before heading out to the countryside for a hike.

"Are you ready?" Arna asked, peeking out of the kitchen.

Just then, they heard the **honk** of a horn: Stefán had arrived. The mouselets grabbed their packs and scurried outside.

"Hey, this is awesome," Pam said, giving the hood of the **SUV** a pat. "You're going to let me take her for a spin, right?"

"**OF COURSE!**" Stefán smiled. "As long as

you're up for it. Our roads are no day at the cheese shop."

Pam grinned. "Don't worry. Cars and I are made for each other!"

A few minutes later, the trunk was full and the **mouselets** were ready.

"But where's Roska?" asked Violet.

"I'm here!" a muffled squeak cried. Roska staggered toward the CAR, her paws filled with two enormouse packages. "We almost forgot the tents."

"Tents?" Colette echoed.

"If I know Uncle Vígmar," Roska explained, "he's journeyed to some isolated place — and there are plenty of those here in Iceland. It's best to be prepared."

Colette sighed. Sleeping in a tent wasn't exactly her dream way to spend a vacation. But she knew it was for a good cause. She gave her friend a paw, and together they found room for the tents in the already-stuffed trunk.

"Are we ready to go?" Stefán asked.

"Go where?" a familiar squeak asked.

"Bryndís! **What are you doing here?**" asked Roska in surprise.

Any news from your uncle?

"I've come to check if you or your sister have received **news** from Vígmar. I'm very worried about the manuscript — *I mean, about your uncle*."

"Unfortunately, no, he hasn't turned up. But we found a message from him. We're worried he's in **DANGER**," Arna replied.

Roska cast a disapproving look at her sister. She wasn't sure they could **trust** their uncle's editor with his **SECRET**.

"What's wrong? It's okay to tell Bryndís what's going on. Uncle trusts her . . . She's his editor!" Arna said.

"So what's **GOING ON**?" asked Bryndís.

"Vígmar left **CLUES** that may lead to the places where he researched his novel. We want to **follow** them and try to reconstruct the story," Stefán explained.

"We're hoping the clues will help us find

him," Arna said.

"**Oh. Well, good luck!**" Bryndís said.

"You'll keep us updated on what happens here, **right**?" asked Colette.

"Yes, if you hear any **news** from Uncle Vígmar, you'll let us know?" Arna added hopefully.

You can count on me!

"What? Oh, sure, of course!" Bryndís replied.

"YOU CAN COUNT ON ME."

WATER FALLING DOWN . . .

It didn't take long to **reach** Gullfoss.

"What's that noise?" Pam asked as she scrambled out of the car. "It's **LOUDER** than the engine of a monster truck."

Roska and Arna **laughed**. "That's no monster truck, but it *is* something monstrously huge! Come check it out," said Roska.

"But first, zip up your **jackets**," Arna added.

After a short scramble along a hiking path, the Thea Sisters and their friends reached a **spot** that left their tails tingling. It was the most majestic **waterfall** they'd ever seen! The water thundered down from over a hundred feet, casting mist and **spray** everywhere. It was truly awe-inspiring.

"This is incredible," Colette murmured, hypnotized by the power of the water in FREE FALL.

"It really is," Stefán agreed. "The waterfall is 105 feet high, and it's fed by the Langjökull Glacier, the second biggest in Iceland."

"No more statistics, please! Thanks to Rattson's clues, I've already got too many NUMBERS spinning around inside my snout," Pam said, laughing. "Anyway, where's this seagull?"

"FOLLOW ME," said Stefán confidently.

The little group made their way down a narrow path. As they scurried along, they were bathed in mist from the waterfall.

"AT LEAST we have jackets," Paulina observed — a moment before getting sprayed

Look at that waterfall!
It's incredible!

by an enormouse jet of water.

Pam laughed. "Guess it was time for you to hit the shower, Paulina."

"**CAREFUL!**" shouted Colette, grabbing Paulina by the paw. The rocks along the path were slick with water and very slippery.

"Go slowly," Stefán advised. "Here in **Iceland**, nature is truly wild. You have to pay close attention to each **pawstep**."

Roska nodded. "Always respect nature. That's a lesson we Icelanders have had in our **hearts** since the time of the Vikings." She reached out a paw and helped Violet move forward carefully.

Meanwhile, the group had arrived at a secluded part of the **river**, where the water fell onto a very low rock.

"The seagull is down there," Stefán **explained**.

"Hang on, mouselets. **Let me go first,**" said Nicky.

Stefán was about to stop her, but Nicky explained, "My country, Australia, is famouse for its wild nature, too. **I know what I'm doing!**"

"Okay," Stefán agreed. "But take my paw, just to be safe."

The mouselets held their **breath** and waited while Nicky and Stefán passed behind the waterfall.

A few moments later, they reappeared. Nicky was holding a small box. "It was under the **ROCK** shaped like a seagull!" she exclaimed.

Arna opened it. Inside was . . .

"A box of **chocolates**?!" Roska wondered.

"Wait. There's no chocolate inside, just this," said Arna, holding up a small key.

"So now we have to find a LOCK," Nicky concluded. She sighed. She was so eager to find her friends' uncle, but figuring out his clues was **harder** than finding a cheese slice in a haystack!

WATER SHOOTING UPWARD

The mice scampered back to Stefán's SUV.

"**Are you sure** it's not just a box of chocolates?" asked Stefán.

"And that you've never seen that key before?" asked Violet.

Arna and Roska **shook** their snouts.

"Does it remind you of a scene from one of Vígmar's books, Violet?" asked Pam.

"No . . . keys inside boxes . . . chocolates . . . It doesn't remind me of **anything**," her friend replied sadly.

"What do you think, Nicky?" Colette asked her friend, who had been silently **looking** at the sky for the last few minutes.

"I think that this country is extraordinary.

Just look at the natural wonder above us! That sky — it seems endless!"

Everyone stopped for a moment and turned their EYES upward. Their problems faded away for a moment as they watched the clouds scudding across the immense Icelandic sky.

"Mouselets, instead of trying to decipher the clue here, why don't we check out another landmark?" Colette suggested.

"Good idea," Paulina said. "When you can't think of a solution right away, the best thing to do is distract yourself and give your thoughts time to percolate."

"But what about our uncle?" Arna murmured, her eyes shining with tears.

Roska put a paw around her sister. "Let's trust our friends," she suggested. "It'll be good to change gears for a moment."

"The most interesting spot nearby is Geysir," Stefán reflected.

"Is that a geyser — hot water shooting out of the ground?" asked Violet.

Stefán smiled. "That's right. The word 'geyser' comes from the name of this place — and you'll soon SEE why."

If the majestic waterfall at Gullfoss had left the THEA SISTERS squeakless, the spectacle of Geysir made them shout in wonder. Jets of boiling water exploded high up into the sky, leaving rainbow reflections.

"The water circulates underground, between the rocks. It's hot because there are many volcanoes in Iceland, and their magma heats up the water. When it reaches the surface, the lack of pressure aboveground makes the geyser explode into a column of

It's a real geyser!

water and steam," Roska explained.

"It's pretty amazing," Pam said.

"Hey, look at that. Is it just me or does that look like our **chocolate** box?!" said Paulina. She was pointing to a **SIGN** for a souvenir shop.

"You're right! I've never seen those chocolates before today, and suddenly we **FIND** both the box and the store that sells them," Roska said. "It can't be a coincidence!"

Colette was one step ahead of her. She was **scurrying** toward the shop at top speed.

"Coco! Where are you going?!" asked Paulina.

"This is no coincidence," Colette called out. "**IT'S A NEW CLUE!**"

AN UNEXPECTED HELPER!

The store was packed with SOUVENIRS: Books, cards, boxes of candy, printed sweatshirts, and hats were stacked all around.

Colette headed to the front, where a rodent with INTENSE blue eyes stood behind the counter.

"Hello. I would like to buy a box of chocolates like the one PAINTED on your sign," she began.

"I don't sell those. They've been off the market for years," the shopkeeper replied.

"Are you sure?" Colette asked.

"Are you suggesting I don't know what I do and do not sell?" the shopkeeper asked, lifting an eyebrow.

By this time, the mouselets and their friends had **CAUGHT UP** with Colette.

"I think we've got the wrong end of the cheese stick," Roska **murmured**.

"Just give Coco a minute," Paulina whispered back. "When she puts her mind

to it, she can get fresh fondue from a block of mold!"

Colette CLEARED her throat. "That's strange, because I'm sure that Inspector Ólafur eats them . . ."

"I DON'T KNOW what you're squeaking about," the shopkeeper replied.

"The author of Inspector Ólafur's adventures wouldn't have made up a CLUE about the chocolates if they were no longer available," Colette went on.

A hint of a smile appeared at the corner of the shopkeeper's snout. "Then someone found his trail?"

Colette smiled triumphantly. "That's right. And I bet you have something for me and my friends!"

"Let's not rush into anything. First you must show me you deserve it. At what

age did Ólafur become an inspector?" the shopkeeper asked.

"**Twenty-four!**" Paulina answered.

"And what was the name of his first dog?"

"**OSCAR!**" said Nicky. "His dog was mentioned in *The Four-Legged Case.*"

"And what's his favorite kind of toothpaste? Mint or licorice?"

There was a moment of silence. Then Colette smiled. "That's a trick question. Neither of them! He only uses homemade toothpaste that his aunt the herbalist prepares!"

The shopkeeper grinned. "Okay, I'll admit it: ***You are true experts!*** I had to be certain I could trust you." He disappeared behind a curtain for a moment and then returned with a **METAL** box in his paws.

"Vígmar and I were school friends," the

shopkeeper explained. "He left this with me three days ago, and he **told me** that if someone came looking for it, I should test them."

Roska took the BOX. "We are Vígmar's nieces," she said. "We're following the clues he left."

"We're afraid he's in **DANGER**," Arna said.

The shopkeeper sighed. "I thought he was **up to something** . . . Please, let me know how things go, okay?"

"We will. You have our word!" Violet replied.

Meanwhile, Roska tried opening the box with the key from behind the **waterfall**.

It was a perfect fit. Inside there was a **USB drive** and a paw-written note.

BLACK TIDE

The THEA SISTERS and their friends couldn't wait to find out more about the BOX'S contents, so they quickly got back in the car. After a few miles, they stopped at a café to examine their new CLUES.

Luckily, Stefán had packed his laptop. He plugged in the USB drive. There was only one FILE on it, simply named "File_1."

"It's a text document," Paulina said, peeking over Stefán's shoulder.

Stefán opened the document, and everyone gathered around to read it.

"Is this what I think it is?!" CRIED Colette.

"It's the first chapter of BLACK TIDE! Our uncle left us his manuscript!" Arna confirmed, excited.

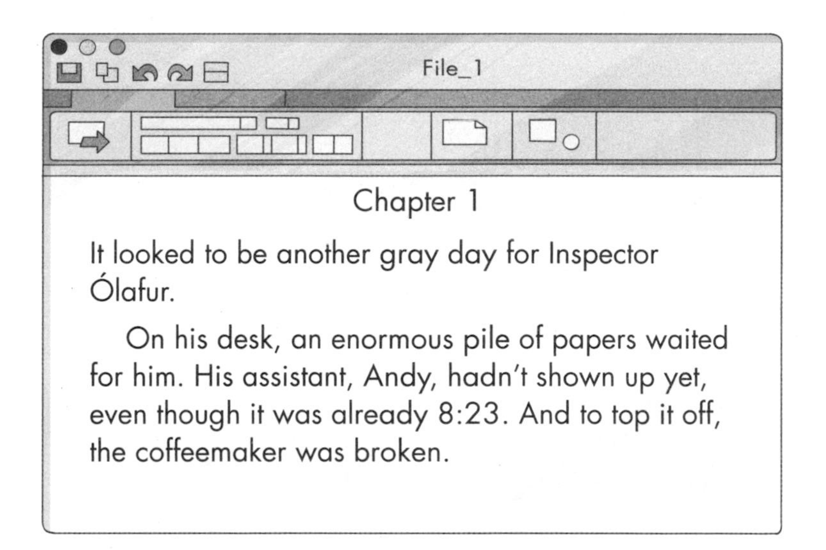
File_1

Chapter 1

It looked to be another gray day for Inspector Ólafur.

On his desk, an enormous pile of papers waited for him. His assistant, Andy, hadn't shown up yet, even though it was already 8:23. And to top it off, the coffeemaker was broken.

"Sssh! Lower your squeak!" Roska said, glancing around nervously.

But the café was DESERTED except for an elderly rodent who was sipping a cup of soup and reading the newspaper.

"If we keep following your uncle's pawsteps, we'll find all the chapters of his *manuscript*," said Paulina.

"Let's look at the latest clue!" said Colette. "Vi, do you have it . . . ? Violet?"

"Huh? Oh yes, of course, here it is . . ." Violet said, blushing. She placed the **note** on the table.

"Were you already **reading** *Black Tide*?" Paulina asked her.

"How could I resist? Even the first lines

are so **compelling** . . .”

“That’s our Violet!” Paulina said. “Once a bookmouse, always a bookmouse.” She grinned at her friend. Then she read the **note** aloud.

In icy water it transforms,
it breaks apart without taking form,
in an ice lagoon that glimmers,
in the sun the statue shimmers.

“**IT’S A RIDDLE!** Arna, you’re usually great at solving these,” Roska said.

Arna took a closer look at the note. “Let’s see. The **ICE LAGOON** could be Jökulsárlón. It’s a lake that stems from a famouse glacier,

and its name means 'glacier lagoon'!"

"And the statue that SHIMMERS. What could that be?" asked Pam.

"I don't know," Arna admitted.

"Let's get GOING. Maybe we'll figure it out on the way," said Pam. "As long as we aren't interrupting anyone's reading, that is . . ."

Everyone looked over at Violet.

"I've already finished," she explained sheepishly. "It was just the first chapter. But now I absolutely must know what happens next! Let's hurry up and get to . . . um . . . Where do we have to go?"

Everyone burst out laughing.

WHERE ICY WATER TRANSFORMS

After a quick snack and a quick review of the first chapter of **BLACK TIDE**, the mice felt more confident about their next step.

As they began the drive to one of the most famouse glaciers in **Iceland**, the THEA SISTERS gazed out the window. Despite the urgency of the matter at paw, they couldn't help admiring the gorgeous countryside.

"Look! There's another waterfall!" Paulina cried.

"And some sheep grazing on that cliff," Nicky added.

"I can see a pool of steaming water . . . with

someone swimming in it!" Colette said.

When they arrived at Jökulsárlón, they found a breathtaking SPECTACLE. Enormouse pieces of clear ice floated on the blue lake. The icy beauty stretched as far as the eye could see.

"Let's look for the sparkling sun . . . the shimmers of the sun . . . What was it?" asked Pam.

"The statue that shimmers in the sun," Colette recalled.

"But I don't see a **single** statue," Nicky observed.

"Did you really think it would be that easy?!" said Roska, smiling. "By now you should know Uncle better than that."

"Good point," Paulina reflected. "But where could someone HIDE a shining statue?"

Stefán stroked his whiskers thoughtfully.

"I know someone who rents boats around here. We could get a RAFT and search the whole lagoon."

Soon the Thea Sisters and their friends were on board a solid raft, slowly cutting through the icy water.

"Wait! I saw something," cried Violet, leaning over the edge of the raft.

"Where?" Pam asked.

"Over there!"

Everyone scanned the area till Nicky exclaimed, "Vi, you saw a seal!"

"Aww, it's so cute!" cried Colette.

"Yeah, but it's not shimmery," Roska said.

Just then, Stefán CRIED, "Look, there's a statue made of ice!"

"It kind of looks like UNCLE VIGMAR," said Roska.

Stefán maneuvered the raft toward the

A statue made of ice!
Oooh!

statue. Then he reached out a paw and **grabbed** a small package stuck between its icy fingers.

Inside there was another **USB drive** and a small bag full of wooden letters.

They had found another clue!

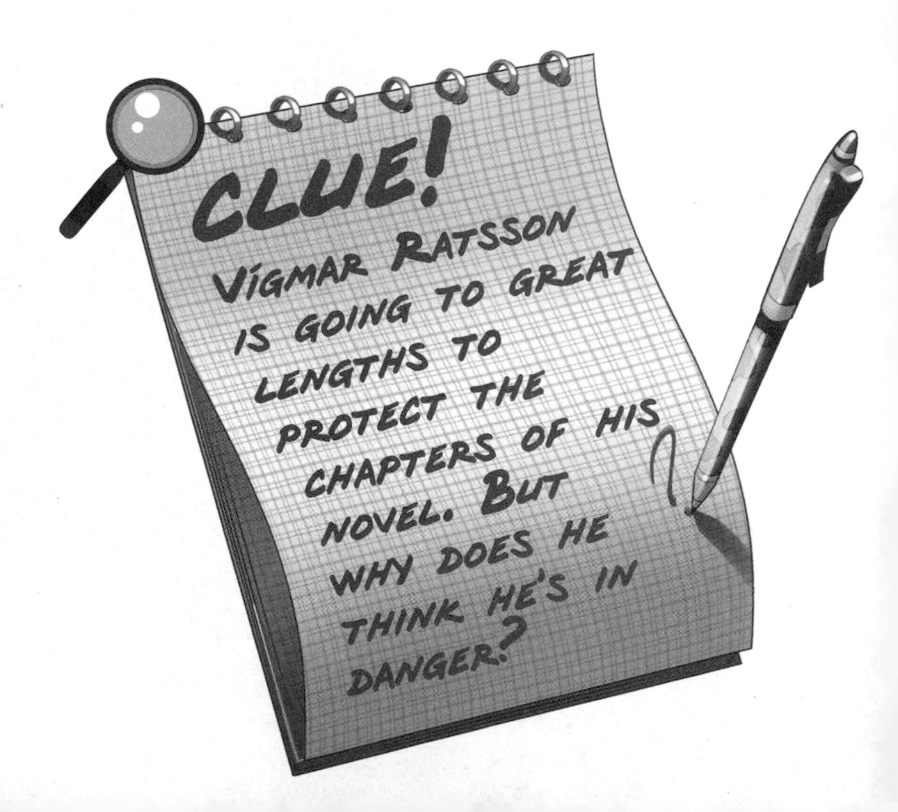

JUST LIKE A NOVEL . . .

"**N . . . Ý . . . V . . . T . . . M . . . A**," Arna read aloud, arranging the letters. Her sister inserted the drive into Stefán's **computer** and opened another chapter of the novel.

Should I read it?

"Violet, why don't **YOU** read it?" Roska asked, anticipating her friend's **desire** to continue the story.

"Are you **SURE** you don't want to?" Violet asked.

Roska shook her snout. "Uh-uh. You're his **BIGGEST FAN**!"

"Let's try to put these **letters** in order," Arna said.

She rearranged them easily to spell the name of a lake, Mývatn.

"It's one of my **favorite** places," Arna said. "It's great for bird-watching."

"It's a bit farther north. We have a long **road** ahead of us," Roska added.

"Okay, then let's get our tails in gear," Paulina declared.

As they drove along, Violet explained the plot of **BLACK TIDE** to the others. "The inspector gets involved in a very complex case. He has to find a missing mouselet, but the clues lead him to yet another **CRIME** I don't understand yet."

"At Mývatn, we'll get the next piece of the puzzle," said Paulina. "I can't wait!"

Once they'd arrived at the **lake**, they divided into two groups. Violet, Colette, Pam, and Arna decided to search the shores,

while Stefán DROVE Nicky, Paulina, and Roska to two nearby landmarks.

The first was a labyrinth of sharp black rocks that resembled the towers of an enchanted castle.

"We're at Dimmuborgir. These are ancient formations of volcanic rock," Stefán explained.

Together the rodents searched for any sign left by Vígmar, but the rocks didn't seem to hold any clues.

The friends moved on to an even more incredible place: Hverarönd, the hot springs, where the reddish earth gave way to pools of boiling water and steaming craters. Unfortunately, they didn't find anything there, either.

The **mouselets** returned to the rest of the group, dragging their tails behind them.

"Did you find anything?" Roska asked.

"Yes . . . a bunch of birds!" Pam replied **bitterly**.

"We're empty-pawed, too. There doesn't seem to be a **single** clue to lead to our

The rock formations of Dimmuborgir

The hot springs of Hveraröndd

uncle or his books," said Arna, sighing.

"His BOOKS!" cried Paulina, lighting up. "Isn't *The Stroke of Midnight* set here at **Mývatn**?"

"Yes!" Violet replied.

"If I remember right, the INSPECTOR swims in the hot springs . . . and he discovers an important clue in the pool," Paulina went on.

"Paulina, are you saying that to solve the mystery, we have to get in the water?" Nicky asked.

Before her friend could respond, Roska and Arna pulled out their bathing suits.

The THEA SISTERS looked at one another and grinned. They weren't about to miss a once-in-a-lifetime experience like taking a thermal bath in Iceland!

"This is fabumouse! There's nothing better

than a nice, relaxing bath," cried Colette, sliding into the large, OPEN-AIR pool.

"Okay, but remember our mission . . ." Violet **reminded** her.

Paulina started splashing from one end of the **pool** to the other. "If this corresponds to the **BOOK**," she explained, "the clue should be hidden under a small bridge . . ."

"Like that one?" asked Nicky, *POINTING*.

A moment later, Paulina had swum to the bridge and pulled a small, tightly sealed package from underneath it. "Just like in *The Stroke of Midnight*!" she cheered.

They had found the next piece of the puzzle!

ON THE HUNT FOR A SCOOP

The THEA SISTERS and their friends climbed out of the pool, shook off their fur, and looked for a good spot to open this mysterious new package.

"Maybe we could find a restaurant?" Pam suggested, her stomach **rumbling** louder than a thunderclap.

"I don't think it's a good idea to open this package in a crowded place," said Paulina. "We're getting close to the end of the story, and this CLUE could crack the case."

"Paulina is right. We should avoid snooping eyes," Nicky added, clutching the package. It was sealed in waterproof wrapping.

"Roska, **remember** when we were little?

We used to camp in this area a lot," said Arna.

"How could I forget?" her sister replied. "Let's **LOOK** for our favorite campsite and sit at one of the tables there to open it."

Fifteen minutes later, the Thea Sisters and their **friends** had scored eight cups of **hot**

chocolate from the campsite café. They gathered around a secluded picnic table and opened the new package.

As usual, it contained a USB drive, which Stefán immediately inserted into his computer. Violet began reading the third chapter of the novel.

"Hmm . . . so *that's* how it is . . ." she muttered, her eyes glued to the screen.

"**How what is? Tell us!**" Nicky urged her impatiently.

"I thought so!" Violet exclaimed. She was so absorbed in her reading that she'd forgotten all about her friends.

"Vi, don't keep us in suspense," Colette said. "Did you find any clues that will lead us to Vígmar?"

"No, though he's truly a master storyteller," Violet said at last. "What started out as a

simple missing-persons case led to shady dealings involving toxic waste that a corrupt INDUSTRIALIST wants to dump into the Icelandic sea!"

"So it's an ecological crime novel," said Stefán.

"Pawsome!" cried Paulina. "Nicky and I are members of the GREEN MICE, an organization dedicated to protecting the environment," she told Roska, Arna, and Stefán.

"Really? Some of their volunteers are coming to help us with a forest-protection project," Stefán said.

GREEN MICE

"OH NO!" Violet squealed.

"What's WRONG, Vi?" Pam asked.

Violet shook her snout. "I'm done reading, but the last part of this chapter is missing.

INSPECTOR ÓLAFUR is about to catch the industrialist who's polluting the sea, but someone is secretly tailing him."

"So the inspector is in danger, just like Uncle Vígmar," Ana said slowly.

"Is there anything else in the package?" asked Colette.

Paulina took the PACKAGE and pulled out a piece of paper with strange symbols on it. "Here's another CLUE."

Pam looked at the note. "I don't understand what these DRAWINGS mean."

Stefán peeked at the note over her shoulder. "These aren't drawings — they're Viking runes!"

The Thea Sisters had no idea what he was squeaking about. "Runes are the alphabet of the ancient rodents who inhabited this land," Stefán explained.

"Stefán loves history. He's been studying the ancient rune alphabet," Arna began to explain.

CLICK!

A loud sound interrupted her.

The mice all turned at once and saw a **SHADOW** escaping into the bushes.

"Someone took our picture!" cried Arna.

Stefán was already in pursuit of the photographer. A few moments later, he returned dragging a familiar rodent by the paw.

"Orri, the journalist?!" Roska exclaimed.

"What's he doing here?" asked Violet.

"He must have followed us," said Pam.

The rodent greeted them casually, trying to pretend nothing unusual had occurred. "Oh, hello, young mice. What a coincidence!"

What are you doing here?
I'm here for my job!

"Don't play innocent," said Arna. "You've been following us. You're still snooping around, trying to get the scoop on our UNCLE!"

The journalist hung his snout. "Well, I thought I'd try to figure out what you'd uncovered. But I didn't FOLLOW you. I was at Mývatn for a different story . . ."

"I don't believe you," Roska said indignantly.

"The important thing is that we've found him," Stefán said. "And now Orri's going to leave us alone, RIGHT?"

The journalist looked around. The Thea Sisters, Roska, Arna, and Stefán were all giving him the same SEVERE look.

"All right, all right." He sighed. "But take my CARD. When you discover something, I want to be the first to publish the news."

LET'S RIDE!

As soon as the journalist had scurried off with his tail between his legs, the friends continued their investigation.

"So, Stefán, you know how to translate this note?" Colette asked.

"I think so," he replied, studying the symbols. "Let's see . . . This says 'Súðavík höfn Odda.' "

"What does that mean?" asked Pam.

"Súðavík is the name of a town in Ísafjörður, an area filled with fjords," Roska answered. "It's in the northwestern part of the island. Höfn is the name of a fishing town in the southeast, but it also means 'PORT.' And Odda is a female rodent's name."

"So perhaps we have to go to one of these

towns and look for Odda at the port," Paulina said.

"And maybe we'll find UNCLE VIGMAR, too," Arna said.

"But which town do we go to?" Violet wondered.

"I think it's Súðavík," Arna said. "Uncle took us there on a trip once when we were little."

"That's true," Roska agreed. "I've never been to Höfn, and I've never heard him mention it, either."

"Then come on," said Stefán. "Let's move those paws!"

As the car made its way along the coast, Arna and Roska exchanged worried whispers.

"We're so close now. You'll see. We'll find your uncle soon," Colette told them.

Roska sighed. "Actually, that's just the problem. Súðavík is still a few hours away."

Arna nodded. "And the sun is already setting. We might arrive in the middle of the night."

"You're right," said Pam. "We need to find a place to spend the night. We can continue in the morning."

After a few miles, Stefán parked the car in front of a quaint little inn. After checking in, the mice sat down for a big dinner of cheese soup. But Roska and Arna were as quiet as mice all evening.

"Keep calm and scurry on, mouselets," said Colette, hugging them. "We'll find your uncle tomorrow, you'll see. Now sleep well!"

The next day, though, the mice woke up to a bitter surprise. Stefán's car wouldn't start.

Pam bent over the engine to FIX IT, but soon she straightened up and shook her snout.

"Bad news, sisters," she said. "The engine is completely BROKEN!"

"Moldy mozzarella!" cried Stefán. "We need to call a mechanic, and that could take hours."

"But we'll lose so much time," Roska MOANED. "Just when we were getting so CLOSE . . ."

Nicky spotted a barn right behind the inn. "I have an idea. Let's go to Súðavík on HORSEBACK!" she cried. "We could take the most direct route over the hills, which might be even faster than a car."

Roska hesitated for a moment. Then she said, "Well, why not? That's actually a genius idea!"

Let's gallop!

Let's go!

Fifteen minutes later, the mouselets and Stefán left the barn on the backs of eight horses. They headed down a path that led northwest.

"**Come on, let's gallop!**" cried Nicky, urging on her horse.

The Thea Sisters smiled. After this morning's quick problem solving,

they were sure they'd crack this mysterious case in no time!

A DOUBLE SURPRISE

About **TWO HOURS** later, the Thea Sisters, Roska, Arna, and Stefán reached Súðavík. They left their horses to graze in a field, as the barn's owner had recommended. He was bringing his horse trailer and would pick them up later. Then the mice headed on PAW toward the town port.

The port was very small, with just one tiny **WOODEN HUT** in front of the dock. There was a fishing boat and one other boat anchored there.

"Let's knock and ask if anyone **knows** an Odda," Violet suggested.

She knocked on the hut's door, but the house seemed EMPTY. No one replied.

Violet turned around, disappointed. "No

luck. There's no one here . . . HEY! LOOK AT THAT!"

One of the boats at the dock had the name ODDA PAINTED in big letters on the side.

"Thundering cat tails!" cried Pam. "It's Odda!"

"Let's check it out. Maybe Uncle Vígmar is there," Roska suggested.

Stefán took her by the paw to STOP HER. "Wait, Roska. It could be dangerous."

She stared at him for a moment, SURPRISED by his caution. Then she shook her snout. "The danger doesn't matter. UNCLE VÍGMAR has been missing for too many days, and now we're so close to finding him! We can't stop to second-guess ourselves."

Stefán smiled. "I don't want to stop you. I'd just prefer to go with you!"

Roska blushed. Together they headed to

ODDA
Wait!

the dock where the boat was docked and crossed the gangway.

They had just reached the deck when a sudden noise made them turn. The Thea Sisters whirled around, and a SHADOW disappeared behind the house.

"Someone is FOLLOWING us," Arna whispered, frightened.

Stefán and Roska SPRANG forward at the same time. Stefán managed to grab the spy by the paw, forcing her to turn around . . .

"Bryndís!"

It was Vígmar Ratsson's editor!

"You . . . you followed us here!" Arna cried, shocked.

"But why?" asked Colette.

"I KNOW WHY!" Roska exclaimed. "You want to get your paws on our uncle's latest

novel, right?" she asked Bryndís accusingly.

Bryndís had been found out. "It's been weeks since your uncle promised to turn in his manuscript, and he hasn't given me anything! So when he didn't show up at the BOOKSTORE, I went to his house . . ."

Colette was startled. "You were the one who searched his house and left it messier than a muskrat den!"

"Yes," Bryndís admitted. "I'm sorry, but I had to do it! After working so hard, I couldn't let his LATEST masterpiece escape me. I didn't find anything at Ratsson's house, so when

you told me that you'd found clues about where your uncle might be, I decided to follow you. And now I **want** all the chapters of the manuscript you found!"

But before anyone could reply, a raspy squeak interrupted them.

"We want the manuscript, too! No excuses, just **PAW IT OVER** . . ."

TRAPPED!

The Thea Sisters and their friends whirled around. They were snout-to-snout with two SKETCHY-LOOKING rats. They were both tall, and one had a thick red beard and a blue-and-green-striped cap. The other had long whiskers and a bandanna on his head.

When Violet saw them, a chill went down her tail. "They look just like the toxic waste traffickers described in Ratsson's BOOK!" she murmured to her friends.

"Then it's all true!" whispered Roska in shock. The two rats stepped closer.

"So you bratty mice are here because of that PENCIL pusher, huh?"

Roska stepped forward. "My uncle isn't a pencil pusher. He's a great writer!"

The rodent with the beard laughed scornfully. "Ha, ha, ha! A great writer! A great **SNOOP**, you mean! He stuck his snout where it didn't belong, and now he's paying the price!"

Arna let out a sob. In a strangled squeak, she asked, "**Wh-where is our uncle?**"

"Yes, we demand to see him!" Roska said.

"Did you hear that, Ulfur? They DEMAND," the rodent with the long whiskers said mockingly.

"You want to see him?" the rat named Ulfur replied. "Well, we can definitely arrange for you to keep him company! But first, give us the manuscript!"

"Never!" shouted Roska.

The bearded mouse grabbed her by the paw. "You will cooperate, mouselet . . ."

Stefán HURLED himself at the bearded rat, determined to free his friend. But the criminal grabbed Stefán by the paw and twisted it behind his back. The other rat grabbed the mouselets and herded them into the abandoned hut. The two rodents closed the door tightly, locking them in!

"If you don't give us what we want, you'll stay locked up. Locked up so that no one will

ever find you! **HA. HA. HA!**" Ulfur shouted from the other side of the door.

"That's what you think!" Roska shouted in reply. She pounded on the door angrily with her paws.

From the back of the **room**, they heard a faint squeak. "Roska? Arna?"

A slender figure emerged. It was a middle-aged mouse with a thick gray beard and **round** glasses.

"Uncle!" cried Arna, running to hug him. "**Are you okay?**"

"Of course," the writer replied. "But what are you doing here?"

The mouselets introduced Stefán and the Thea Sisters to their uncle and quickly told him how they'd managed to **find him**.

"We've been following the trail you left," said Arna.

My nieces!
Uncle!

Colette nodded. "Your CLUES were as compelling as the plots of your novels!"

"Thank you, my dears. If I had known the **DANGER**, I would never have led you here," the writer replied despairingly.

"Don't WORRY about us, Uncle," Roska said. "You'll see. Together we'll find a way to get out of here."

"That's right!" Violet agreed. "Who are these TWO RODENTS who captured you? Can you tell us?"

Vígmar Ratsson took a deep breath and began his tale . . .

DANGEROUS INVESTIGATIONS

"When I began writing my new novel," Vígmar explained, "I planned to write an ecological mystery, which would begin with the mousenapping of a young rodent . . ."

Violet nodded. He was talking about the first chapter of the book, which she and her friends had found at Geysir.

"And then . . . ?" asked Roska, eager to know how her uncle had ended up in the paws of these shady rats.

The writer was quiet for a moment. "I began to research to make sure my tale was realistic. As I was reading up on ecological issues here in Iceland, I came across some **newspaper articles** that described

strange phenomena: fish and birds getting **SICK**, the growth of **unusual** algae . . ."

"All the classic symptoms of ocean pollution," cried Nicky. Thanks to the **GREEN MICE**, she knew a lot about this **subject**.

Ratsson nodded. "Exactly! The articles were by journalists in different areas of the country, but I started to realize there was a **CONNECTION** between the events. Something very **SERIOUS** was going on! The first episode of **contamination** was reported near Gullfoss, so I started my investigation there."

"But, Uncle, you should have called the **POLICE**!" Roska cried.

"Yes, I know. But I didn't have any proof, except for **my instincts**, and that wasn't enough for an investigation. I wanted to leave a trail just in case, so I wrote a **letter**."

"Of course," said Arna. "We found it in the **BOX** hidden in the refrigerator."

The writer sighed. "I never thought anyone would actually use it. If I had realized I'd be leading all of you into trouble, **I NEVER WOULD HAVE LEFT IT**."

"Don't say that, Uncle. That letter put us on the **RIGHT TRACK**," replied Roska. "Go on. What happened next?"

"At Gullfoss, I looked for **information** about that story, which led me to Ulfur and Olaf," Ratsson continued.

"The two rats who locked us in here!" cried Roska **ANGRILY**.

Her uncle nodded. "I followed them and discovered that they worked for a large oil company that's responsible for the **contamination** of the sea."

"And as your investigation continued, you kept writing your **novel**, right?" Violet asked.

"Yes. I found myself weaving together reality and fiction, constructing a story **SIMILAR** to the one happening around me," the writer replied.

"And to make sure that your story didn't

fall into the wrong paws, you decided to HIDE IT on the various stages of your journey," Violet concluded.

"Along with the CLUES to follow your investigation," added Nicky.

Ratsson smiled. "You're very clever."

"Thanks," Roska said. "But now we need to get OUT of here!"

The mouselets examined the HUT'S interior. Unfortunately, it didn't have windows, and there was only a small bed, a table, and a broken chair inside.

Stefán gave the door a few shoves. "The lock

is on the other side, and this wood will never give way!" he said.

Everyone shared a tense look. They were **trapped** in the paws of two dangerous criminals!

Roska began pacing BACK and FORTH like a cat outside a mousehole. "How do we get out of here?!"

A USEFUL PAIN IN THE TAIL

Nicky, who couldn't stand being in **CLOSED-IN** spaces, said nervously, "We **really** have to find a way out soon . . ."

"I shouldn't even be here!" squealed Bryndís.

"If you hadn't been so nosy, you *wouldn't* even be here!" Roska sputtered, **irritated**.

"What do you mean, Roska?" her **UNCLE** asked.

"We don't have time to rehash everything," Colette said. "Let's try to come up with a plan."

Colette sighed. "Stefán, it's pointless to try to knock down that door. You said yourself that it's made of heavy WOOD. You'll just end up hurting yourself."

The ratlet STARED at her. "But I'm not doing anything," he replied.

Colette didn't understand. Then she turned to look at the door.

Again they heard a heavy noise, followed by almost inaudible squeaking.

"Did those two sewer rats come back?" Arna murmured.

Colette strained her ears. "It sounds like someone trying to force open the lock . . . but who?"

Suddenly, they heard a sharp click, and the

door slowly began to **OPEN**.

"**Hello . . . ?** Anyone in here?"

A moment later, the door had opened a crack, and a very familiar snout appeared.

"Orri?!" the mouselets cried.

"Shhh!" he said, putting a paw to his lips. "You don't want them to find us, do you?"

What are you doing here?!

"What are you doing here?" asked Roska.

The journalist turned **redder** than a calico cat. "Well, you told me to go away . . . but I didn't. I kept **following** you. When I saw those two rats bring you in here, I knew you were in **TROUBLE**. So I decided to try to help you. My truck is **hidden** behind some bushes nearby."

Roska threw her paws around the journalist. "You were right not to listen to us! **THANK YOU!**"

Thank you!

FREE?

When Orri realized he'd found the missing writer, he almost fainted with excitement. "The one time I act for purely selfless reasons, I uncover a sensational scoop!"

"That should teach you a lesson," Colette said. "Thea says a true journalist must always act out of love for the truth, not out of self-interest."

"You're right," Roska said. "But our biggest priority right now is getting out of here!"

Vígmar and the others tried to slip out, but their path was blocked. Ulfur and Olaf were right outside the HUT.

"Now we can't escape," Stefán murmured, pulling the door shut again.

"Don't close the door!" Orri said. "Let's

wait, and when they go away we can sneak off . . ."

Bryndís shook her snout. "We can't just let those criminals **GO FREE**."

The others looked SURPRISED, but Vígmar smiled. "Well said, Bryndís. I see you've chosen the right side."

Bryndís **nodded**. "I was wrong before — I shouldn't have been trying so hard to get my paws on your *manuscript*. I should've been trying to find you!"

"How are we going to slip past those thugs? They've already managed to trap us once

without using force," Stefán reflected.

There was a moment of silence, and then Paulina squeaked up. "Mr. Ratsson, remember the ending of *August Storm*?"

The writer's eyes lit up. "That's just what we should do!"

"What in the name of cheese are you squeaking about?" asked Pam.

"In that book, Ólafur found himself in danger — and managed to make the criminals fall into their own TRAP," Paulina explained.

"Tell us what you have in mind," Stefán said.

"First of all, we have to lock ourselves back inside," Paulina said.

That suggestion made everyone a little

nervous. But Vígmar **agreed** with Paulina. "Listen to what we need to do . . ."

A few minutes later, the mouselets and their friends put their plan into action.

"**Hey you, out there!**" the mouselets shouted. Everyone **battered** the wooden door with all their strength.

Finally, they heard Ulfur and Olaf approaching.

Orri ran to hide beneath the table, deep in the hut's **SHADOWS**.

"Who's squealing?" the two **criminals** thundered from the other side of the door. "That won't make us let you go!"

"We decided to paw over the manuscript you want so much," **Roska** replied.

"Why did you change your mind?" Ulfur asked uncertainly.

"**We want to get out of here!**" Roska replied.

Don't do it!

"Don't do it! Don't give it to them!" shouted Vígmar.

Ulfur and Olaf had no idea this was all an act. "**FINALLY!** Now give us that book . . ." Olaf began, opening the door.

But Bryndís was waiting just inside the doorjamb. She hit him over the snout with an old **frying pan** they'd found on the table.

"Hey, what . . ." said Ulfur, following Olaf.

Stefán stuck out a PAW to trip him, and Ulfur ended up flat on his back with his paws in the air. Pam and Nicky tied him up with a blanket from the bed.

"**GREAT!** Now let's get out of here," said Roska.

But Olaf got up and **STAGGERED** toward her. Arna grabbed the broken chair

Got you!
Stop right there!
Heeeelp!

and used it to trap the **crook**. He was completely immobilized. "You play with the rat, you get the tail!" she cried.

"Thanks, **SIS**! You're so brave," cried Roska.

"It's not over yet," Arna replied, taking the **CELL PHONE** out of Olaf's pocket. "The police will find this very interesting!"

Soon the mouselets and their friends were safely outside.

Their adventure was finally coming to an end!

LIKE A FAIRY TALE

Once the police had taken their statements, everyone but Ulfur and Olaf was free to go. The THEA SISTERS, Roska, Arna, Stefán, Vígmar, and Bryndís all climbed into Orri's truck. GREEN fields and high cliffs, BLACK rocks and red earth, clouds of steam erupting from the ground, and bright blue water flew by as they drove.

"We've been here almost a week, but I'm still in awe of this gorgeous countryside," Paulina commented.

"Me, too," said Colette. "It's so strange, but so beautiful!"

"And to think there are rodents who want to pollute it . . ." Violet reflected.

"The important thing is that we've spoiled

What an amazing place!

their plans," Roska said with a smile.

"Yeah, all thanks to your uncle," Pam concluded.

Vígmar had been following their conversation from the front seat. "No, no, the CREDIT is all yours. You investigated together, and you refused to let anyone or anything get in your way."

"Are you saying that we're almost as good as INSPECTOR ÓLAFUR?" Colette asked.

"Oh, no, not at all!" Vígmar cried. Colette **blushed** to the roots of her fur. But the writer quickly added, "You're much, much better!"

"Because we're a real team!" Roska said.

"Friends together, mice forever!" Pam cheered.

"Now that the police know what's going

on, they'll stop those **criminals**, right?" Arna asked.

"Of course. With the proof I gathered for my **BOOK**, those sewer rats are sure to end up behind bars," Vígmar confirmed.

"But I still have one question," Violet said. "How does your book end?"

The writer laughed. "Well, I haven't written the ending yet. But that won't be a problem. I've found lots of inspiration from our adventure."

"And so Ólafur's latest story will end just like the fairy tales we loved when we were little . . . happily ever after!" Arna **said**, smiling.

THE FINAL ENIGMA

A few **MONTHS** had passed since the Thea Sisters' journey to **Iceland**. But the mice would never forget it. And they often thought about their **INVESTIGATION** with Roska, Arna, and Stefán.

"Mouselets," said Pam, balancing her plate on her paw in the academy's cafeteria, "hasn't it been a while since we've heard from Roska and Arna?"

"**Do you think they've forgotten us?**" Violet asked.

"No way, that's ***impossible***! There must be something going on," said Nicky.

"Isn't **BLACK TIDE** about to hit shelves?" Paulina asked. "They're probably very busy."

"It would be great to get to attend a real

reading for it," said Violet.

"Well, we'll be able to read it once it's published here on Whale Island . . . even though we already know the story so well!" Colette said, winking at the others.

Then the friends started chatting about their classes and their clubs, and they forgot all about Vígmar Ratsson's book.

They remembered it a few hours later, though, when there was an unexpected visit from Mercury Whale, the Island's mailmouse. He scampered into the classroom right in the middle of Professor Rattcliff's literature lecture.

"Mercury, to what do we owe the honor of your presence?" the professor asked.

"I have an urgent package for the THEA SISTERS," replied the mailmouse as he deposited a BOX on Colette's desk.

"Professor, may we open it?" she asked.

Her teacher sighed. "Well, since my lesson has already been interrupted, we might as well satisfy our curiosity."

When the Thea Sisters opened the package,

they discovered five brand-new books!

"It's five copies of the same book. These are first editions of BLACK TIDE!" Violet cheered. "Roska and Arna sent them!"

There was also a letter in the package. "It's a note from the author!" cried Nicky. "'To my five dear friends, who to the third become true characters!'"

"*To the third?* But what does that mean?" asked Connie, studying the note.

"He may be a great writer," commented Alicia, "but his letters don't make any sense."

The Thea Sisters smiled. Vígmar hadn't lost his love of riddles and puzzles!

"Five . . . to the third* . . . Something tells me that on PAGE 125 there's a surprise for us!" Paulina whispered.

Sure enough, on page 125, something

* This is a mathematical operation called *powers*. "Five to the third" means to multiply five three times, 5 x 5 x 5, which equals 125.

The new book!

special appeared: the names of **five characters** . . . Paulina, Nicky, Violet, Pamela, and Colette!

"Vígmar Ratsson put you in his **BOOK**?!" asked Ruby in disbelief.

"**WOW!**" Zoe said.

The other students gathered around the Thea Sisters, curious to see the paw-written letter from the famouse author.

"Um, ahem . . ." Professor Rattcliff cleared her throat.

"**Sorry, Professor** . . ." Colette said.

"It's okay," the teacher replied. "I'm a big *fan*, too."

"Really?!" Violet asked.

"Of course! I love to **read**, and the plots

of Ratsson's books are nearly perfect," Professor Rattcliff replied. "Hmm. Perhaps this is a good time for a QUICK LESSON ABOUT MYSTERY NOVELS. Can anyone tell me the most important elements of a good mystery?"

At once, five paws shot into the air.

The THEA SISTERS grinned at one another. They couldn't wait to share the story of their **ADVENTURE** in Iceland with their classmates!

Don't miss any of these exciting Thea Sisters adventures!

Thea Stilton and the Dragon's Code

Thea Stilton and the Mountain of Fire

Thea Stilton and the Ghost of the Shipwreck

Thea Stilton and the Secret City

Thea Stilton and the Mystery in Paris

Thea Stilton and the herry Blossom Adventure

Thea Stilton and the Star Castaways

Thea Stilton: Big Trouble in the Big Apple

Thea Stilton and the Ice Treasure

Thea Stilton and the ecret of the Old Castle

Thea Stilton and the Blue Scarab Hunt

Thea Stilton and the Prince's Emerald

Thea Stilton and the Mystery on the Orient Express

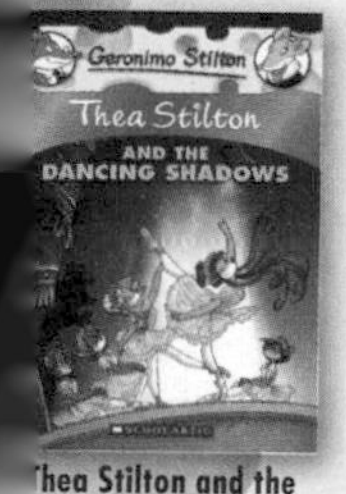

hea Stilton and the Dancing Shadows

Thea Stilton and the Legend of the Fire Flowers

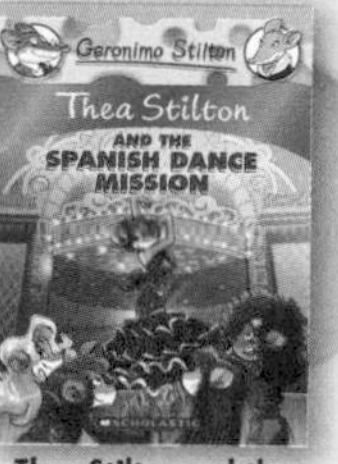

Thea Stilton and the Spanish Dance Mission

Thea Stilton and the Journey to the Lion's Den

Thea Stilton and the Great Tulip Heist

Thea Stilton and the Chocolate Sabotage

Thea Stilton and the Missing Myth

Thea Stilton and the Lost Letters

Thea Stilton and the Tropical Treasure

Thea Stilton and the Hollywood Hoax

Thea Stilton and the Madagascar Madness

Thea Stilton and the Frozen Fiasco

Thea Stilton and the Venice Masquerade

And check out my fabumouse special editions

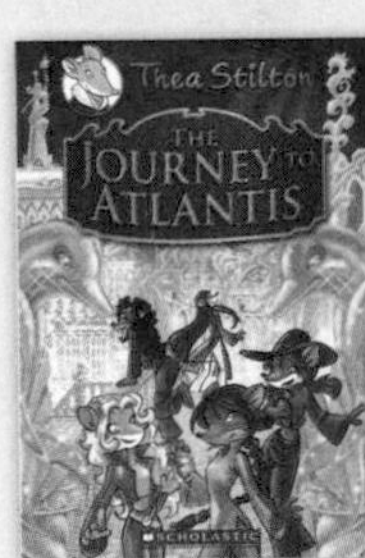

THEA STILTON: THE JOURNEY TO ATLANTIS

THEA STILTON: THE SECRET OF THE FAIRIES

THEA STILTON: THE SECRET OF THE SNOW

THEA STILTON: THE CLOUD CASTLE

THEA STILTON: THE TREASURE OF THE SEA

THEA STILTON: THE LAND OF FLOWERS

Be sure to read all my fabumouse adventures!

#1 Lost Treasure of the Emerald Eye

#2 The Curse of the Cheese Pyramid

#3 Cat and Mouse in a Haunted House

#4 I'm Too Fond of My Fur!

#5 Four Mice Deep in the Jungle

#6 Paws Off, Cheddarface!

#7 Red Pizzas for a Blue Count

#8 Attack of the Bandit Cats

#9 A Fabumouse 'acation for Geronimo

#10 All Because of a Cup of Coffee

#11 It's Halloween, You 'Fraidy Mouse!

#12 Merry Christmas, Geronimo!

#13 The Phantom of the Subway

14 The Temple of the Ruby of Fire

#15 The Mona Mousa Code

#16 A Cheese-Colored Camper

#17 Watch Your Whiskers, Stilton!

#18 Shipwreck on the Pirate Islands

My Name Is Stilton, Geronimo Stilton

#20 Surf's Up, Geronimo!

#21 The Wild, Wild West

#22 The Secret of Cacklefur Castle

A Christmas Tale

#23 Valentine's Day Disaster

#24 Field Trip to Niagara Falls

#25 The Search for Sunken Treasure

#26 The Mummy with No Name

#27 The Christmas Toy Factory

#28 Wedding Crasher

#29 Down and Out Down Under

#30 The Mouse Island Marathon

#31 The Mysterious Cheese Thief

Christmas Catastrophe

#32 Valley of the Giant Skeletons

#33 Geronimo and the Gold Medal Mystery

#34 Geronimo Stilton, Secret Agent

#35 A Very Merry Christmas

#36 Geronimo's Valentine

#37 The Race Across America

#38 A Fabumouse School Adventure

#39 Singing Sensation

#40 The Karate Mouse

#41 Mighty Mount Kilimanjaro

#42 The Peculiar Pumpkin Thief

#43 I'm Not a Supermouse!

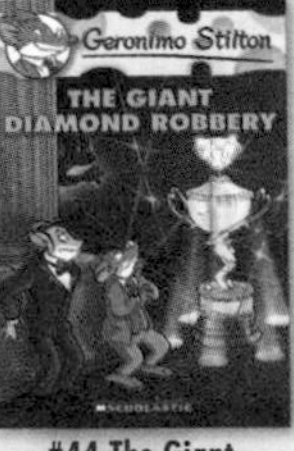

#44 The Giant Diamond Robbery

#45 Save the White Whale!

#46 The Haunted Castle

#47 Run for the Hills, Geronimo!

#48 The Mystery in Venice

#49 The Way of the Samurai

#50 This Hotel Is Haunted!

#51 The Enormouse Pearl Heist

#52 Mouse in Space!

#53 Rumble in the Jungle

#54 Get into Gear, Stilton!

#55 The Golden Statue Plot

#56 Flight of the Red Bandit

The Hunt for the Golden Book

#57 The Stinky Cheese Vacation

#58 The Super Chef Contest

#59 Welcome to Moldy Manor

The Hunt for the Curious Cheese

60 The Treasure of Easter Island

#61 Mouse House Hunter

#62 Mouse Overboard!

The Hunt for the Secret Papyrus

#63 The Cheese Experiment

4 Magical Mission

#65 Bollywood Burglary

The Hunt for the Hundredth Key

#66 Operation: Secret Recipe

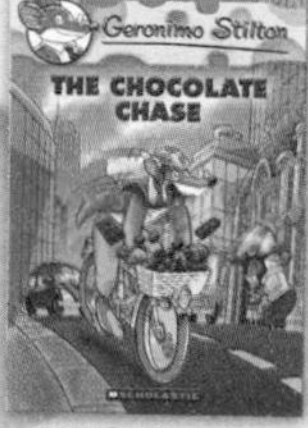

#67 The Chocolate Chase

Don't miss any of my adventures in the Kingdom of Fantasy!

THE KINGDOM OF FANTASY

THE QUEST FOR PARADISE:
THE RETURN TO THE KINGDOM OF FANTASY

THE AMAZING VOYAGE:
THE THIRD ADVENTURE IN THE KINGDOM OF FANTASY

THE DRAGON PROPHECY:
THE FOURTH ADVENTURE IN THE KINGDOM OF FANTASY

THE VOLCANO OF FIRE:
THE FIFTH ADVENTURE IN THE KINGDOM OF FANTASY

THE SEARCH FOR TREASURE:
THE SIXTH ADVENTURE IN THE KINGDOM OF FANTASY

THE ENCHANTED CHARMS:
THE SEVENTH ADVENTURE IN THE KINGDOM OF FANTASY

THE PHOENIX OF DESTINY:
AN EPIC KINGDOM OF FANTASY ADVENTURE

THE HOUR OF MAGIC:
THE EIGHTH ADVENTURE IN THE KINGDOM OF FANTASY

THE WIZARD'S WAND:
THE NINTH ADVENTURE IN THE KINGDOM OF FANTASY

THE SHIP OF SECRETS:
THE TENTH ADVENTURE IN THE KINGDOM OF FANTASY

THE DRAGON OF FORTUNE:
AN EPIC KINGDOM OF FANTASY ADVENTURE

Meet CREEPELLA VON CACKLEFUR

Geronimo Stilton, have a lot of mouse
iends, but none as **spooky** as my friend
REEPELLA VON CACKLEFUR! She is an
chanting and MYSTERIOUS mouse with a pet
t named **Bitewing**. YIKES! I'm a real 'fraidy
ouse, but even I think CREEPELLA and her
mily are AWFULLY fascinating. I can't wait
you to read all about CREEPELLA in these
mouse-ly funny and **spectacularly spooky** tales!

The Thirteen Ghosts

#2 Meet Me in Horrorwood

#3 Ghost Pirate Treasure

#4 Return of the Vampire

#5 Fright Night

#6 Ride for Your Life!

#7 A Suitcase Full of Ghosts

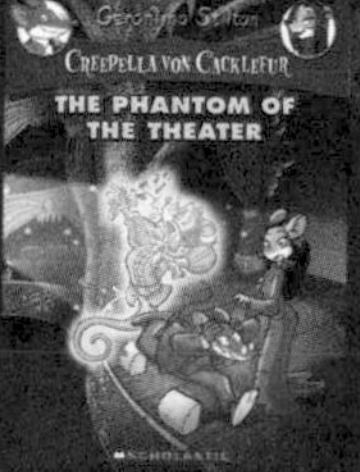

#8 The Phantom of the Theater

#9 The Haunted Dinosaur

THANKS FOR READING, AND GOOD-BYE UNTIL OUR NEXT ADVENTURE!

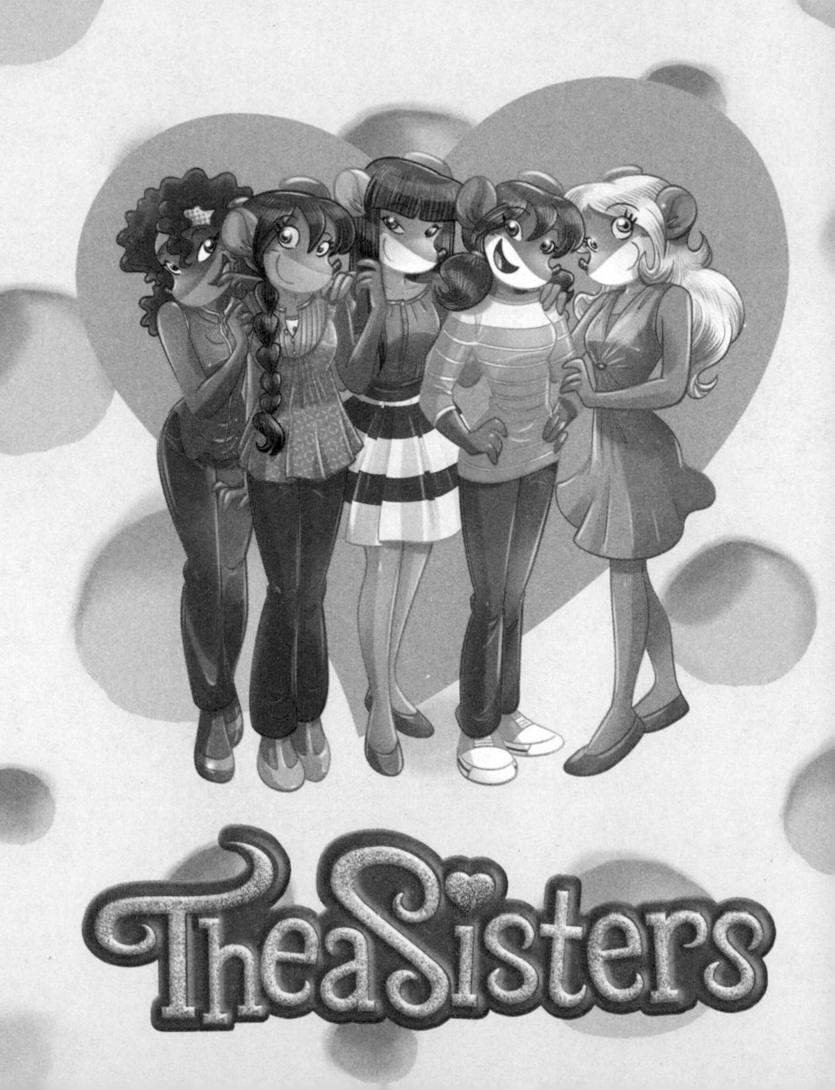